Heather Fell in the Water

Words by
Doug MacLeod

Pictures by
Craig Smith

ALLEN & UNWIN
SYDNEY · MELBOURNE · AUCKLAND · LONDON

Heather was a little girl ...

...who always fell in the water.

She didn't mean to do it.
She didn't enjoy it.
But she fell in the water nearly every day,
especially when she was wearing her good clothes.

Heather's parents were worried for her safety,
so they made her wear water wings all the time.

One day her parents took her to visit a farm.

Heather fell in the water.

They took her to an art gallery.

Heather fell in the water.

They took her to a Japanese tea house.

Heather fell in the water.

Heather started to hate the water,
and she was sure that the water felt the same about her.

Why else would it make her fall in all the time?

When the children at school
had to take swimming lessons,
Heather refused to go.

'The water hates me,'
she said.

But Heather's parents told her she really should learn to swim,
in case she fell in some *deep* water one day.

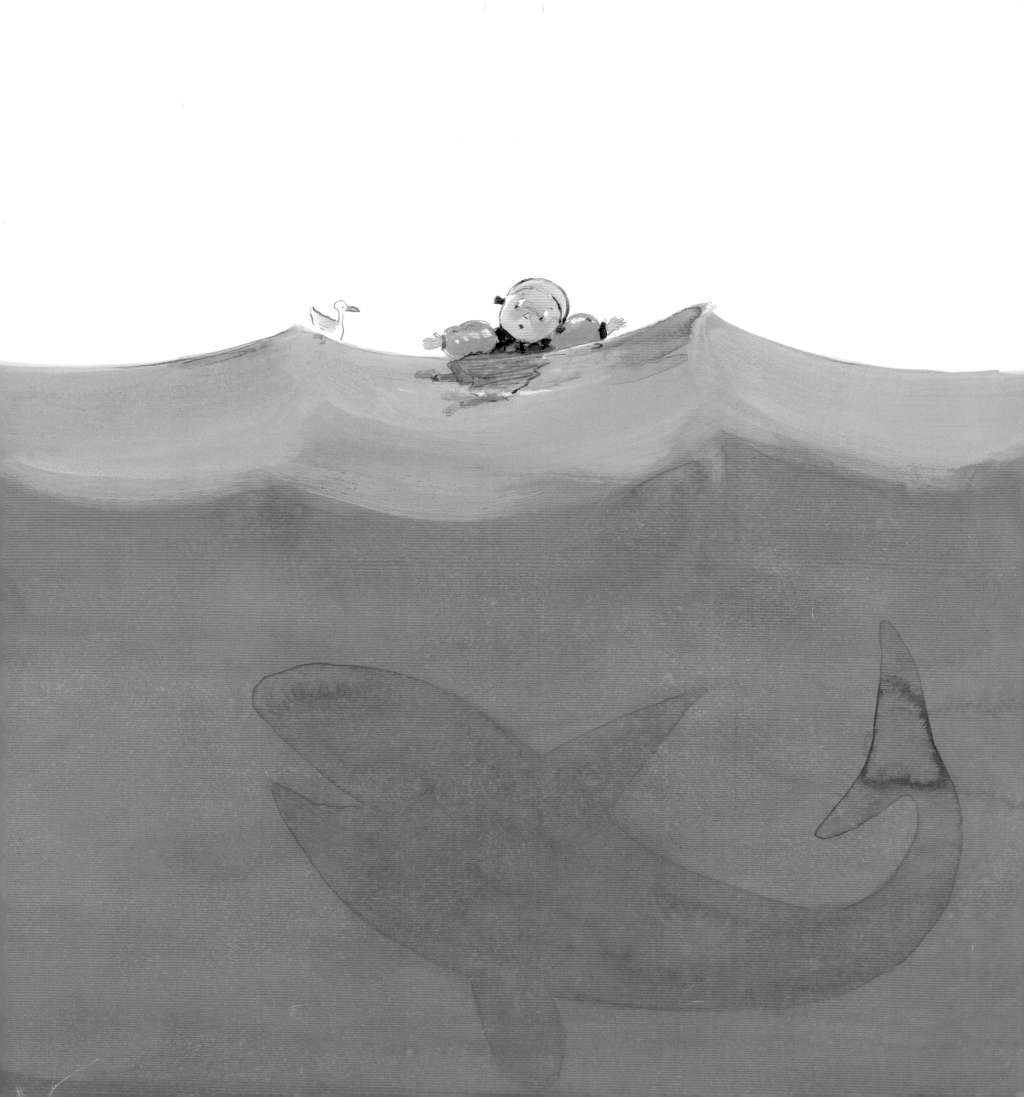

So they took Heather to the swimming pool.
They held her hands as Heather tiptoed into the shallow water.
Then they gently let go.

Heather didn't fall over!
Instead she sat down. It felt nice.
She asked her parents if she could
take off her water wings.
They said she could.

Heather moved her arms through the water.
That felt nice, too.

She wriggled and kicked her legs.
That felt the nicest of all.
Heather spent a whole morning
enjoying the water with her parents.

Heather realised the water didn't hate her.
It *loved* her. That was why it kept making her fall in.
It wanted to be with her.

So Heather made a bargain with the water.
She promised she would learn to swim,
if it stopped making her fall in all the time.

The water kept its bargain.
Heather stopped falling in the water.
Instead, she would put on her bathing suit
and climb bravely into the pool all by herself.

Later, Heather would *dive* in.

Later still, Heather competed
in the school swimming sports.

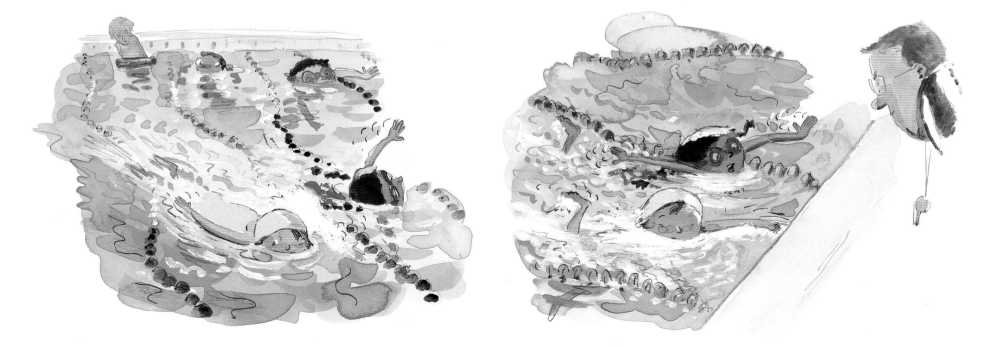

Heather was the champion.
Her parents were so proud that
they jumped up and did a dance.

Then they fell in the water.

About the Author

Doug MacLeod is one of Australia's leading writers of comedy, and has been part of the creative teams that have produced popular TV shows like *Kath and Kim*, *The Comedy Company* and *Fast Forward*. He has written 26 books, several of which have been illustrated by Craig Smith, including the award-winning bestseller *Sister Madge's Book of Nuns*. This story is completely true: his little sister Heather really did always fall in the water.

About the Illustrator

This story reminded Craig Smith of the time he slipped off a rain-sodden log into a running creek as a kid, and realised he was losing the struggle to stay up. Luckily he survived, and went on to illustrate over 370 picture books, junior novels and educational readers – approximately 8500 published drawings. About 300 of these drawings (the best ones) have been in collaborations with Doug MacLeod.

First published in 2012

Allen & Unwin
83 Alexander Street
Crows Nest NSW 2065
Australia
Phone: (61 2) 8425 0100
Fax: (61 2) 9906 2218
Email: info@allenandunwin.com
Web: www.allenandunwin.com

A Cataloguing-in-Publication entry is available from
the National Library of Australia – www.trove.nla.gov.au

ISBN 978 1 74237 648 6

Cover and text design by Bruno Herfst & Craig Smith
Set in 17.5 pt Dolly
Colour reproduction by Splitting Image, Clayton, Victoria
This book was printed in May 2012 by TWP SDN BHD, TAMPOI, No. 89 Jalan Tampoi, Kawasan Perindustrian Tampoi, 80350 Johor Bahru, Malaysia.

10 9 8 7 6 5 4 3 2 1

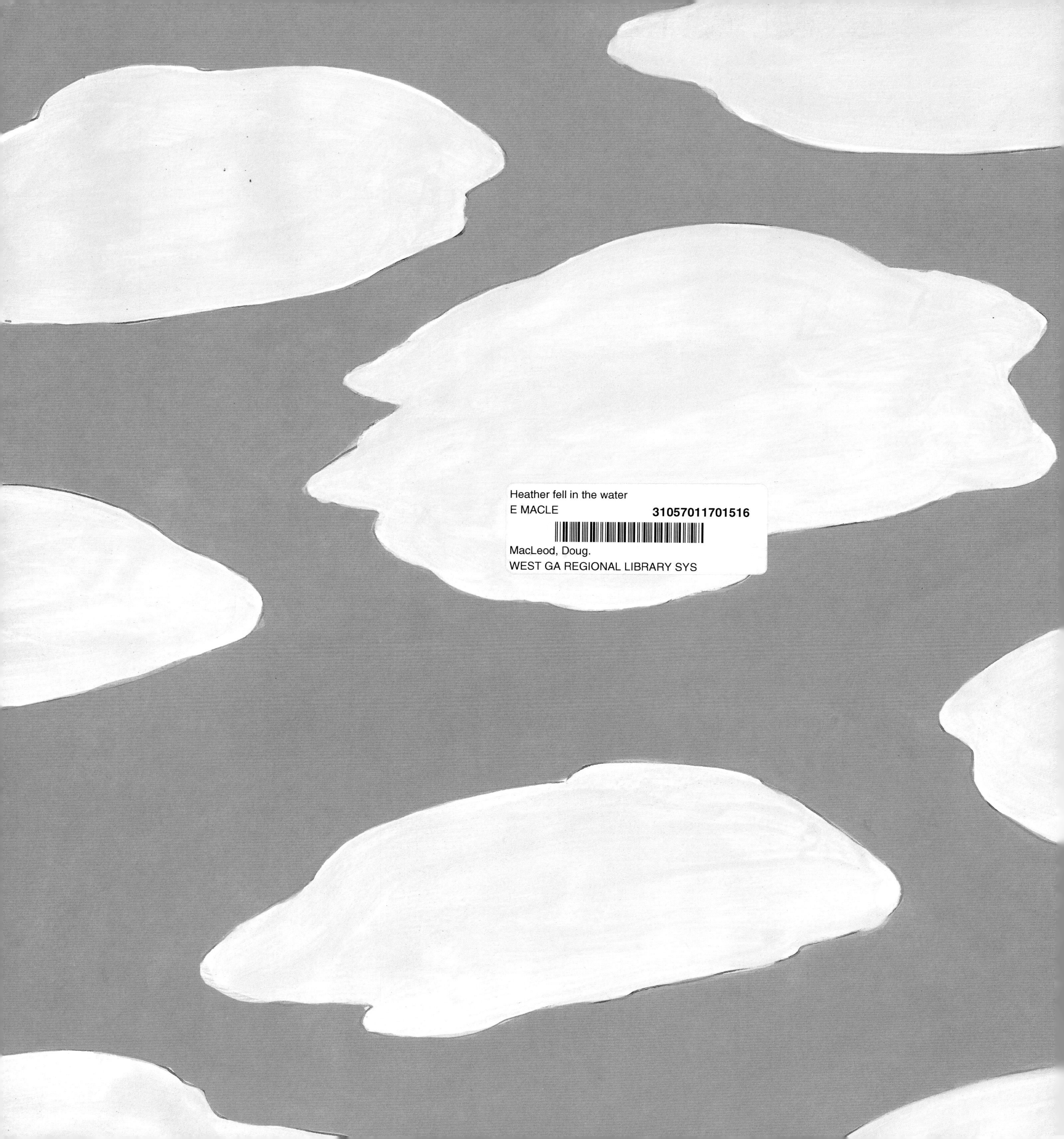